When the Anger Ogre Visits

Wisdom Publications • Boston

To José Asunción.
To Lugrit, loving redhead.
To the trees, who teach us to live with joyful stillness,
and to the fires that provide us with warmth.

Wisdom Publications
199 Elm Street
Somerville, MA 02144 USA
www.wisdompubs.org
© 2015 Andrée and Yvette Salom
All rights reserved.

Library of Congress Cataloging-in-Publication Data
Salom, Andrée.
  When the Anger Ogre visits / by Andrée Salom ; illustrated by Ivette Salom.
    pages cm
    Summary: A child learns that anger is a natural and manageable part of life.
    ISBN 1-61429-166-7 (cloth)
    [1. Stories in rhyme. 2. Anger—Fiction. 3. Meditation—Fiction. 4. Relax-
    ation—Fiction.] I. Salom, Ivette, illustrator. II. Title.
    PZ8.3.S1735Wh 2015
    [E]—dc23
                                    2014020587

ISBN 978-1-61429-166-4   eISBN 978-1-61429-183-1

19 18 17 16 15
 5 4 3 2 1

Artwork by Ivette Salom. Cover and interior design by Philip Pascuzzo.

Wisdom Publications' books are printed on acid-free paper and meet the guidelines for permanence and durability of the
Production Guidelines for Book Longevity of the Council on Library Resources.

Printed in the PRC.

When the Anger Ogre Visits

by **Andrée Salom**

Illustrated by
Ivette Salom

When the
Anger Ogre
visits in a
frenzy
with a frown,

What can we do to
calm the Ogre down?

Invite the
Anger Ogre,

invite it in for tea.

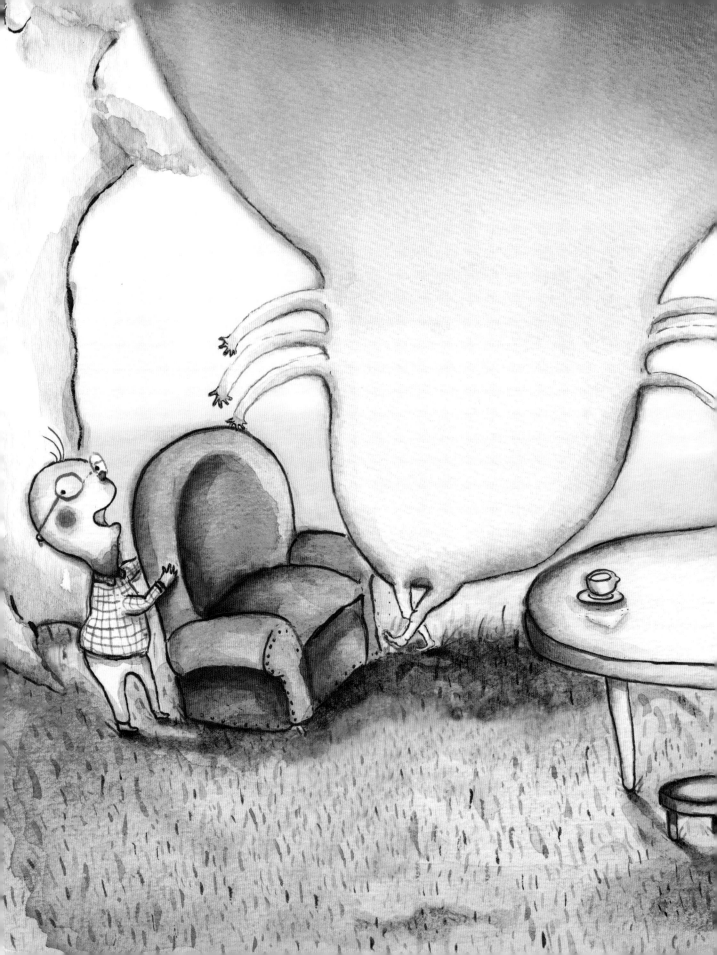

Choose a cozy spot
for the Ogre by a tree.

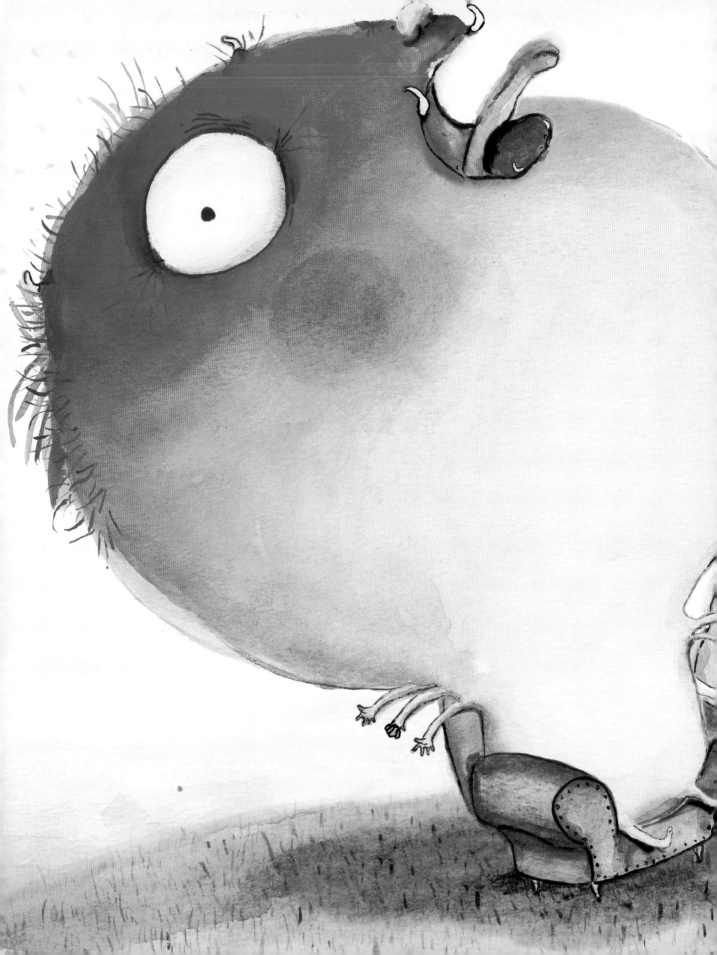

If the Anger Ogre

is still swollen, tense, and hot,

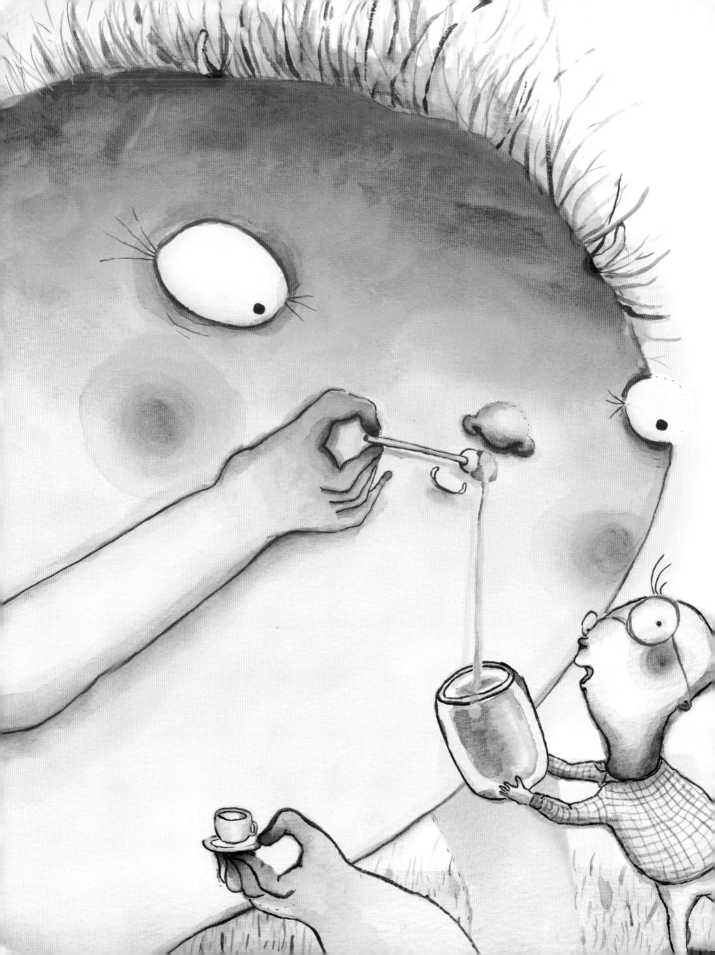

offer it some honey
of the sweetest kind you've got.

Breathe slow and very deeply

before you sip your tea.

Relax as
you imagine

you're afloat
upon the sea.

Relax
your tongue.

Relax
your toes.

Relax
your belly.

Relax
your nose.

Relax your ears
so you can hear
the sound of your breath,
always so near.

As you pay attention,
the Ogre will change form.

What at first seemed scary

becomes **friendly**, **gentle**, and **warm**.

If I stay calm, I act more kind,
because I can see my feelings and mind.

The Anger Ogre
visits everybody's lives!

Just remember
to be **patient**
whenever it arrives.

Next time it comes
a-knocking,

you'll know just
what to do.

Invite the
Anger Ogre

to **relax** and
breathe with you.

A Note for Grown-Ups

Children naturally learn about personal emotions by observing the behavior of those around them. It is important for adults to provide a positive example of how to relate to difficult emotions in a consistent way. This book is meant to facilitate communication and understanding about the anger that arises inside each one of us.